# Born t

adapted by Tish Rabe from a script by Patrick Granleese
illustrated by Christopher Moroney

 A GOLDEN BOOK • NEW YORK

Seussville.com    pbskids.org/catinthehat    treehousetv.com

ISBN: 978-0-307-93080-4
Library of Congress Control Number: 2011928319
Printed in the United States of America    10 9 8 7 6 5 4 3 2 1
Random House Children's Books supports the First Amendment and celebrates the right to read.

"Flick the Jiggermawhizzer!"
said Nick. "And let's fly
our Thinga-ma-jigger
up into the sky!

Get ready for takeoff.
Let's get on our way.
What kind of adventure
should we have today?"

"Adventure?" the Cat said.
"You'll soon get your wish!
Today we will swim with
a very strong fish.

You'll meet my friend Sam,
and we'll have lots of fun.
She's a salmon, and she'll
show us how salmon run!"

"Do they run," said Nick,
"like we run down the street?
How can they do that
without any feet?"

"Salmon run when they swim
against the current," said the Cat.
"Fish have to be strong
to swim upstream like that."

"Press the Shrinkamadoodle
and we'll get so small . . .

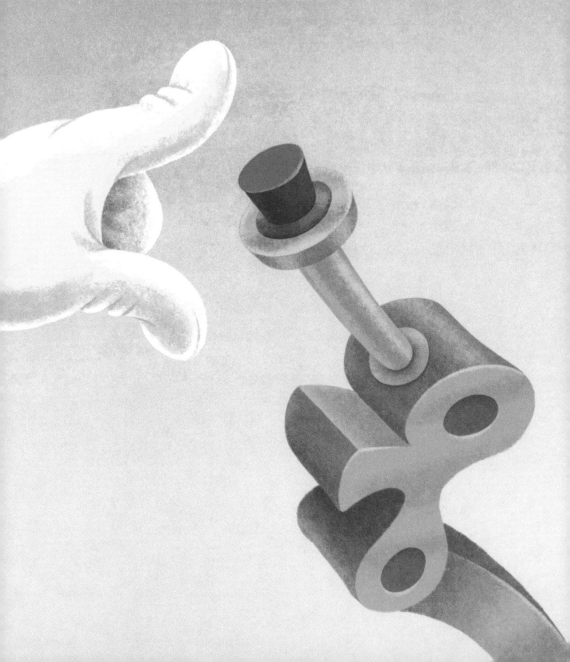

. . . we will not frighten
the salmon at all."

"Hello!" said Samantha.
"Just look at me run.
I leap out of the water
and flash in the sun!"

"Watch out!" cried Sally.
"I see a bear paw!
It's the biggest bear paw
that I ever saw!"

"Hey, bear!" yelled Sam,
and then she cried, "Whee!
There's no way that you
will ever catch me!"

"Excuse me," said Nick.
"Can you move, Mr. Bear?
We're swimming upstream
and we need to get there!"

"A boy fish? A girl fish?
A fish with a hat?
I've seen some strange things,"
said the bear, "but not that."

"Look out!" cried Sally.
"Do you see up ahead?
It's a big waterfall!"
"Flip your tails!" the Cat said.

"We made it!" said Sally.
"Sam! Where are you?"
Then they heard Sam
gently calling, "Yoo-hoo!"

"I'm here," whispered Sam.
"And I'm happy to say
I just laid my eggs.
I laid them right away."

"My beautiful eggs
are also called roe.
And soon all my eggs
will be starting to grow!

They'll grow to be salmon,
and one day, you'll see,
they'll make the same journey
upriver as me."

"Goodbye, Sam," said Sally.
"We had lots of fun.
Thank you for showing us
how salmon run."

"Swimming upstream," the Cat said,
"is what salmon do.
If you were a salmon . . ."

". . . you'd swim upstream, too."